Samuel Barstow Sumner

A Poem

Delivered at the Reunion of the Forty-Ninth Regiment, Massachusetts

Volunteers...

Samuel Barstow Sumner

A Poem
Delivered at the Reunion of the Forty-Ninth Regiment, Massachusetts Volunteers...

ISBN/EAN: 9783337268985

Printed in Europe, USA, Canada, Australia, Japan

Cover: Foto ©Andreas Hilbeck / pixelio.de

More available books at **www.hansebooks.com**

A POEM

DELIVERED AT THE

Reunion of the Forty-Ninth Regiment

MASSACHUSETTS VOLUNTEERS,

AT

Pittsfield, Mass., May 21, 1867.

BY

SAMUEL B. SUMNER,

LIEUTENANT-COLONEL OF THE REGIMENT.

WITH NOTES AND AN APPENDIX.

SPRINGFIELD, MASS.:
SAMUEL BOWLES & COMPANY, PRINTERS.
1867.

POEM.

How strange a thing is memory: as I gaze
This night on comrades of those fruitful days,
When armed cohorts thronged on every hand,
And war's alarms and thunders shook the land;
I am not here,—but backward, far away,
My inmost thoughts and recollections stray,
And bygone scenes are passing in review,
Which, haply, I may reproduce to you.

And first, Camp Briggs[1] attracts my gaze; the spot whereto we
rallied,
When forth from peaceful hearths and homes, as raw recruits
we sallied;
When, having stumped the county o'er, for men to aid the nation,
We undertook the rudiments of martial education.

And first, there came the "Allen Guard,"[2] with Captain Israel
Weller,—
A whilom three-months Sergeant, and a funny, whole-souled
feller;
With Clark and Francis for his aids, he fired the opening gun;
And straightway boldly issued General Order Number One!

Then Garlick, Plunkett, Sumner, Train and Morey, followed fast ;
Then Parker, Shannon, Rennie, and then Weston came, the last ;
And so, ten goodly companies encamped upon the green,
While tents and shanties multiplied, enlivening all the scene.

O then 'twas drum-beat, morn and night, and tramp, tramp, all
    the day,
And not a little arduous toil, and very little play ;
The boys complained of homesickness ;—the discipline seemed
    hard ;
And ever and anon, at night, the rascals ran the guard.

What stunning dress-parades we had, at every close of day,
When all the Pittsfield gentry came to witness the display ;
When Captain Weller put us through the exercises fine,
And R. R. Noble, Adjutant, went strutting down the line!

And then, what everlasting drills, and marches up and down,
Eliciting the compliments of all the belles in town ;
And as we marched in column on, about a score abreast,
Good Lord ! how Plunkett's towering form loomed up above the
    rest ![3]

Pete Springsteen[4] furnished us with "grub," according to our
    means.
The beefsteak tasted mighty good, and eke the pork and beans.
Our appetites were glorious, and we minded not the odds,
And quaffed our coffee, piping hot ; 'twould kill at forty rods !

Of Pittsfield hospitality, I hardly need remind ;—
This grand old town, whose people were so generous and kind ;
Where many a mansion, with the warmth of welcome, was aglow,
As, through the "witching hours," we tripped "the light fan-
    tastic toe."

And here, the pensive muse would pause, in sadness to deplore
The death of Sarah Morewood, who shall greet us here no more.
Deep on the white entablature of memory, we record
Her virtues, yielding now, we trust, exceeding rich reward.[5]

At first, the clear October days were mild and warm enough ;
But, by and by, the nights grew cold, and winds blew chill and
      rough ;
The guard-house was a populous and thriving institution,
And the number of our rank and file betrayed a diminution.

We shall not soon forget the day, when orders came to leave,—
To pack all up for Worcester, and go that very eve ;
Our tents were struck, our knapsacks slung,—and then,—lo, and
      behold !
Our train came not, and there we stood, a'shivering in the cold !

On the horrors of that dreadful night, I need not here to dwell,—
The men were all disgusted, and the officers, as well ;
But, what with show of pistols, and of handcuffs, brought from
      town,
And sharing with the men the "gloom," we kept their temper
      down.

The welcome morning dawned at last ; the tardy train arrived ;
We gave Camp Briggs a parting cheer ; our spirits quite revived ;
With many a benediction from many an anxious friend,
Away we sped ;—and so I bring this chapter to an end.

And now, at Camp Wool, Worcester, we tarried for awhile.
We came at night, and travel-worn for many a weary mile ;
That snow-storm you'll remember, and the wintry winds that blew,
And the hospitable snow-drifts that we had to stumble through !

But the comfortable barracks, and the host of generous friends
We found down there in Worcester, soon made complete amends ;
And the drilling-grounds were spacious, and the winds began to
  lull ;
Oh ! after traveling farther, we sighed for Old Camp Wool !

And Colonel Ward,[6] who held command, and afterwards who died
A hero's death, we here recall with sorrow, yet with pride ;
A courteous gentleman was he ; a soldier true and brave ;
Long let memorial flowers bloom above his honored grave !

And here it was we organized ; and for our leader, chose
A private at the war's outbreak—a General at its close.
He needs no cheap insignia now— of eagles, or of stars,—
For his badges of nobility are honorable scars.[7]

The "Bay State"[8] was a famous place for sociable resort,
Where Captain Shannon took by storm the grand Piano Forte ;
Where Weller improvised the dance, and Doctor Rice grew
  mellow,
And spun his yarns, which made him out—a devil of a fellow !

The ladies came in troops, to do our necessary stitching,
To glad us with their charming smiles, and manners so bewitch-
  ing ;
In truth, I deem it very sure, had we much longer tarried,
Each bachelor would then and there have been decoyed and
  married !

But orders came to move again ;—again we watched in vain
From day to day, the coming of the transportation train ;
We lingered through Thanksgiving, and were happily surprised
By a dinner which those same dear creatures quickly improvised.

Next day we took the Norwich cars, and then the "Commodore,"
A steamboat staunch, which bore us straight to old Manhattan's
    shore;
And so, one drizzly morning, fatigued and hungered all—
We stretched our line across the Park, before the City Hall.

The barracks up in Franklin Street, became our next resort,—
A place to study insect-life of every phase and sort;
We tarried but a week or so,—but plenty long enough,
For the best accommodations there—to draw it mild—were
    "rough."

Behold us on Long Island next, at Union Course encamped:
The ground was wet, and so our feet and ardor both were damped;
However, we contrived to live and flourish passing well,
For Hiram Woodruff's was hard by, and Snedeker's Hotel.

And here it was we lingered for quite a length of time,
And many a day experienced the roughness of the clime;
At East New York we had a row, and the Sutler grew so mean,
The boys upset his apple-cart, and smashed up his machine.[9]

But by and by they placed our boys,—their comfort to increase,
Where trotting nags had quartered in the piping times of peace;[10]
And here we stayed, and here we drilled, and kept our snug abode,
And marched our soldiers back and forth, along the smooth
    plank road.

And now, a large detachment was assigned for provost work,
In picking up deserters in the City of New York—
Our boys resolved themselves into a Vigilance Committee,
To watch that mythic "Elephant," that stalks about the city.

At length there came an order, to our most unfeigned joy,
To embark our troops for Dixie, on the steamer Illinois;
We set sail in high feather, but, arrived off Sandy Hook,
A feeling slightly singular our senses overtook.

A disposition seized us, to keep the vessel's side,
And cease our conversation, and only watch the tide;
We found some strange attraction the briny surge beneath,
And many a mouth was wide agape,—and Kniffin lost his teeth!

And when we reached Cape Hatteras, our symptoms were re-
    doubled,
And many a fellow's stomach with dreadful qualms was troubled;
O ever since, when I desire my veriest foe to be
With heaviest penance visited, I wish him out at sea!

We gained at length the South-west Pass, of Mississippi's stream,
And once more, of smooth waters and green fields, began to
    dream;
But our voyage seemed prosecuted beneath a luckless star,
And our ship was over-freighted, and we couldn't cross the bar.

We telegraphed to New Orleans, and soon with joy espied
The Yankee boat, "New Brunswick," at anchor alongside;
She bore us up the river, and beneath the clear moon's light,
The soil of Louisiana regaled our gladdened sight.

Next morning, as we trod the deck, with interested eye,
We gazed on fine plantations, as we swiftly floated by;
The sweet abodes of peace they seemed, nor could we from afar,
Discern as yet the havoc wrought by fratricidal war.

And now, upborne in heaven, the Day-king held his throne,
And in the glorious sunlight, a hundred steeples shone;
There sat the Crescent City on the river's eastern shore,
O how unlike the City it had been in days before!

Its levees all deserted for miles along, save where
A federal transport lay in wait for orders, here and there;
While in mid-stream the gunboats lay, with ever threat'ning frown,
And iron fingers pointing tow'rds the proud but conquered town.

And here we ate fresh oranges, and, after noon sailed on,
A few miles up the river, to encamp at Carrolton, —
A place, by no means such as that for which our hopes were
    looking,
The most attractive thing to us, was Madame Schraeder's
    cooking.

But here we met the Thirty-First, and glad enough were they
To welcome us, so lately come from Berkshire homes away;
And many a spot we talked about, where we would like to peep in,
Of dinners that we used to eat, and beds we used to sleep in.

We took some trips to New Orleans along about those days,
And studied its geography, and learned its devious ways;
And dined at the St. Charles Hotel, and looked at octoroons,
But, others having been and gone, we brought away no spoons.

For Baton Rouge we started next, — the night was chill and dark,
It took us until past midnight, our baggage to embark;
The Major's horse fell overboard; we bivouacked on the shore,
And the Colonel vowed those cook-stoves should cumber us no
    more!

We floated up the river the following day and night,
Till we saw afar the State House, with its massive walls of white;
And the Hospital we wot of, and the Arsenal, all standing
Along the river's eastern shore, the noble stream commanding.

And here we joined the 1st Brigade, in Augur's famed Division,
And carried on our strict routine with order and precision;
And here, I recollect, we all financially were *busted*,
But Train and Morey came across some sutlers there, who trusted!

And here, until the 14th day of March, we lay at ease,
When General Banks conceived a plan, with force and arms to
      seize
The stronghold of Port Hudson;—here let the Muses rest,
I'll sing that olden ballad; it will aid our memories best.

THE PASSAGE OF THE MONTESINO."

Banks, of Shenandoah fame,
      By the Crescent City swore
That Port Hudson, on the river,
      Should defy his might no more.

By the Crescent City swore it,
      And sent without delay,
An order to his Chief of Staff,
      To summon his array.

He summoned to him Farragut,
      And gave him orders sealed;
Then, girding on his armor,
      With his staff he took the field.

Attend ye to the story,
  Which I will now relate ;
It happened in the Lowlands
  Of Louisiana State.

T'was on a cool March morning,
  That we our steeds bestrode ;
And, just as day was dawning,
  Struck the Bayou Sara road.[12]

We crossed the Montesino
  By plank bridge, and pontoon ;
And halted for the bivouac,
  Three hours after noon.[13]

We plucked the rails from off the fence —
  Of boards there were but few, —
And spread our scanty shelter tents,
  To shield us from the dew.

The air was filled with squeal of pigs,
  And cackle of the geese ;
While stalwart oxen lost their hides,
  And simple lambs, their fleece.[14]

And now the night was falling,
  Soon rose the evening star ;
And through the deep'ning twilight,
  Gleamed camp-fires from afar.

But hark ! what noise arises !
  This night we sleep no more ;
For the tide of battle surges
  On Mississippi's shore ![15]

And now, an aide from Chapin,—
　　The Driller of Brigades—[16]
An order brings to form the line
　　In haste, without parades.

Upon his own black stallion
　　Sat the gallant Brigadier ;
And he called to him the Colonel,
　　And he whispered in his ear ;

" Our army has attacked the Fort,
　　And been repulsed ;"—they say—
" In haste o'ertake the Forty-Eighth,[17]
　　And homeward lead the way ! "

The road is blocked with wagons,
　　The darkness settles down ;
But swiftly marched the FORTY-NINTH,
　　In silence·back to town.

The FORTY-NINTH marched swiftly ;
　　But swifter far than they,
Beneath their feet, the Forty-Eighth
　　Let no grass grow, that day.

Their Colonel had been ordered
　　By General Banks, they say—
To hold the Montesino,
　　And keep the foe at bay.

　　*　　　*　　　*　　　*

　　*　　　*　　　*　　　*

　　*　　　*　　　*　　　*

The Bayou Montesino reached,
  No foe was there discovered ;
And silence was the deity,
  That o'er the valley hovered.

Ah, then the gallant Forty-Eighth
  Did mighty deeds of valor ;
And courage on each countenance,
  Assumed the place of pallor.

And now their Colonel, homeward bent —
  Their manly zeal arouses ;
" Press on, brave boys, and seize and hold
  Our lumber and cook-houses ! " [18]

And so for many a weary mile,
  In toilsome march, we find them ;
Before them were their household gods ;
  The FORTY-NINTH behind them !

And now, a short half mile ahead,
  The old camp greets their vision ;
And each indulges sweet foretaste
  Of sleep and dreams elysian.

But look ! behind, a cloud of dust
  Our eyes are now discerning ;
It cannot be ; — it is, it is
  An order for returning ! [19]

The Reverend Chaplain — worthy soul —
  Had trotted on before ;
And so he did not hear his flock,
  How dreadfully they swore !

The sun was near his setting —
   The clouds betokened rain ;
When, having reached the Bayou,
   We pitched our tents again.

And now, in all their fury,
   The elements are roaring ;
And down in copious torrents,
   The watery flood is pouring.

O orange groves, and palm-trees !
   O land of milk and honey !
Where zephyrs were so very soft,
   And skies so bright and sunny ;

We thought to spend a winter here,
   Should fortune so decree it,
Would be the thing : — but, on that night,
   We really could'nt see it !

All o'er the deeply-furrowed field,[20]
   The waters rose so high,
Our boys could neither make their beds,
   Nor keep their powder dry.

The guns with rust were covered o'er,
   And many a luckless wight
Began to think his chance was slim,
   If forced into a fight.

But if he dared to try his piece,
   And if it chanced to go ;
He had to stand at " shoulder arms,"
   For half a day or so.[21]

At Bayou Montesino,
  For six long days we stayed,
To tempt the Rebel foemen
  Our precinct to invade.

We gobbled up their sugar,
  We licked their syrup fine ;
And longed to lick the rebel,
  Who dared approach the line.

But only to O'Brien's[22] gaze,
  And the gallant cavaliers,
Who hailed from " Little Rhody,"
  The enemy appears.

In vain did General Dudley
  His whole Brigade deploy,
And execute maneuvres,
  The rebels to decoy.

For, as that famous army
  Aforetime, marched in vain ;
So, Dudley did go forward,
  And bravely back again.[23]

Of all that week's adventures,
  The muse lacks words to tell,
" I never see that ! " she says with " Jock,"
  And sighs "Ah! well! well! well!"[24]

At length there came an order ;
  On dress-parade t'was read ; —
T'was General Banks who sent it —
  Now what do you think it said?[25]

" My valiant boys ; take courage !
   Our object is attained ;
Your cue is to be jubilant,
   For victory has been gained.

" Perhaps you deemed it ' running,'
   The morn you were so fleet ;
But the truth is, you were making
   A ' masterly retreat !'

" You see, I only wanted —
   While Farragut passed through
The gauntlet on the river —
   That you should hollo ' Boo ! ! !'

" I came, a week beforehand,
   To Baton Rouge, you know ;
And had a very grand review ;—
   But that was all for show.

" And now, my boys, I thank ye,
   For gallant deeds ye've done ;
Go back to camp, and rest ye
   On the laurels ye have won.

" And in the long hereafter,
   Be this your glorious boast ;—
' We went with Banks's army
   To Port Hudson . . . . . almost !' "

Then there came a thrilling order in the following month of May,
To take by storm Port Hudson, with ardor to essay ;
It was a fearful struggle, and the Muse forbears to dwell
On that momentous conflict, and the fate which there befell.[26]

For memory will remind us of the gallant boys who died,
While with us there contending, fighting bravely, side by side ;
Who sleep in nameless graves afar beneath that Southern sod,
And whose souls were thence uplifted to the presence of their God.

O if no other impulse moved our hearts to gather here,
To hold one brief communion, with each recurring year ;
Our duty still were plain enough, since haply we survive,
Their sacrifice to count, and keep their memories alive.

O such a brotherhood as ours, we shall not find elsewhere,
And ours are obligations that we never may forswear ;
The warm fraternal flame within our breasts can ne'er expire,
For our initiation was THE BAPTISM OF FIRE.

From the threshold of Eternity, amid the battle's din,
We did hardly meet dismissal, as our brothers entered in ;
They have crossed the stream to where the fields with lasting
        verdure smile,
And we, upon its hither shore, are lingering yet awhile.

Yet not unscathed did we escape the battle's angry storm,—
I stand surrounded here by many a scarred and shattered form ;
The grim Death-Angel, hurling forth his missiles thick and fast,
Gave some of us the tokens of his presence as he passed.

Then let us praise the God of Hosts, whose overruling power
Did shield us, and deliver us in that portentous hour ;
Nor let those heroes moulder there, unhonored, and unwept,
In that mysterious sleep which peradventure we had slept !

   Thus, Brothers, in numbers less brief than intended,
     I have sung, as my impulses moved me ; and now,
   Ere the harp be unstrung, and its minstrelsy ended,
     Let us banish the sadness that sits on each brow.

3

The conflict is over ; and vict'ry, descending,
　Is perched on the Banner, so proudly we bore ;
And the white dove of Peace its glad presence is lending,
　And we list to the clamor of battle no more.

I have sung of our perils by land and by water,
　And glimpses of by-gones have sought to unfold ;
Of scenes of enjoyment, of hardship, of slaughter ;
　Yet how much after all there remaineth untold !

But while memory lasts, though our heads became hoary,
　The events we were part of we shall not forget ;
But to our children's children shall narrate the story,
　While with tears sympathetic, their eyes shall be wet.

And as time shall roll on, let us happily gather,
　Now and then one more glance retrospective to cast ;
With a fondness and longing unlessened, but rather
　More deep, as our years recede into the past.

And now, let the generous cup be o'erflowing
　With grateful libations, potential to cheer ;
The rapture of social enjoyment bestowing,
　As we strengthen the ties of our fellowship here !

NOTES.

1. CAMP BRIGGS, Pittsfield, so named in honor of Brigadier General H. S. Briggs.

2. The "Allen Guard," a militia company in Pittsfield, named after Hon. Thomas Allen, who had contributed largely to its organization and support, was the first Company of the Forty-Ninth to go into camp. It established itself at Camp Briggs on Sunday, September 7, 1862, which was the day when the Thirty-Seventh Regiment left it for the seat of war.

3. The Forty-Ninth was known wherever it went as "the Regiment with the tall Major." Major Plunkett was six feet six, in his uniform, and although he has relapsed into peaceful avocations, it was noticeable at the late reunion, that his shadow had grown no less.

4. Peter Springsteen, whilom landlord of the United States Hotel, Pittsfield, furnished rations for officers and men, when the camp was first established, and accompanied the Regiment South, as its sutler.

5. Mrs. Sarah A. Morewood, late of Pittsfield, now deceased, was a lady of ample means, and proportionate generosity. The Thirty-First and Thirty-Seventh Regiments while encamped at Pittsfield had received many favors at her hands, but the Forty-Ninth were especially indebted to her for many acts of kindness and attention. Before leaving Pittsfield every officer was presented by her with a portfolio with writing materials, in convenient form for camp use, and also a copy of the Scriptures, and a number of miscellaneous books. The whole Regiment was the recipient of her hospitality on many occasions, at Pittsfield, and while in barracks in New York, and in camp on Long Island.

6. Colonel George Ward commanded the camp at Worcester when the Forty-Ninth arrived. The Fifty-First Massachusetts Regiment was also there. Colonel Ward had been in active service, and the artificial leg which he wore testified that he had been to the front. He afterwards returned to active duty, and eventually fell in battle.

7. Major General Bartlett was in the Junior Class at Harvard when the war broke out. He enlisted as a private for the three months' campaign; then he became Captain in the Twentieth Massachusetts, and was acting much of the time

while in that Regiment as a Field Officer. At the battle of Ball's Bluff he showed great bravery and skill, and succeeded in bringing off from the field a small remnant of his men, crossing the river himself in the last boat, after seeing his command safely out of the clutches of the enemy. While before Yorktown he received a wound in his leg, requiring amputation above the knee. Subsequently he was appointed Commandant of the post, at Camp Briggs, and although an entire stranger to the officers of the Forty-Ninth, so favorably impressed them, that they chose him as their Colonel. He served with the Regiment, and was severely wounded in the attack on Port Hudson, May 27, 1863. After the Forty-Ninth was mustered out, he became Colonel of the Fifty-Seventh, and served under Grant in the long campaign of 1864–5 against Richmond. He was wounded at the battle of the Wilderness, and for his bravery promoted to be Brigadier General. At the attack on Petersburgh, at the time of the explosion of the mine, General Bartlett was captured, and was a prisoner in the hands of the enemy for some time. At the close of the war, he was brevetted a Major General, at the age of twenty-five, a most merited compliment, most fitly bestowed at the termination of so remarkable and brilliant a career.

8. The Bay State Hotel, Worcester, was the place where we went occasionally to get a "square meal," and have a social time.

9. The allusion here is by no means to our old friend Springsteen, but to the mercenary rascal who contracted to feed the troops on Long Island *by the job*, and undertook to serve the boys with rations of rancid pork, swill soup, and beef that was "an infringement of Goodyear's patent for Vulcanized Rubber."

10. The barracks in the rear of Snedeker's Hotel, consisted of the stalls which had been used for trotting horses, in connection with the races at Union Course. The names of many celebrated nags were posted up in the stalls which they had respectively occupied, and the use to which these accommodations had come to be appropriated, was matter of considerable remark and merriment.

11. This ballad, "The Passage of the Montesino," was written at the time and on the spot, and contains scintillations of more than one genius. Several officers had a hand in its production. In fact, nearly half of it was written before I was invited to take a share in the intellectual effort necessary for its completion. The several authors would prefer not to publish their names, but I am bound to state that the Regiment could boast a good deal of undeveloped poetical talent. The ballad was read by a great many within and without the Regiment at the time it was written, and I am glad to put it in shape for preservation, after eliminating some local allusions and hits the printing of which would be matter of doubtful propriety.

12. The road leading out of Baton Rouge, northerly towards Port Hudson, some twenty-five miles distant.

13. The Bayou Montesino is a small stream or creek, about six miles North of Baton Rouge. The place where we "halted for the bivouac" is some miles further north.

14. The "gobbling" done by our men on that expedition, was something tremendous. It was strictly forbidden in orders from Head-quarters, but hunger knows no law, and officers were obliged to wink at some depredations upon private property in the enemy's country, especially as an occasional rare bit thereby found its way into their own mess.

15. There was heavy cannonading during the night, as Farragut was attempting to pass the batteries on the River, and did succeed in passing Port Hudson with the Flag-ship Hartford, and the Albatross. The head of our column was also near enough to Port Hudson to make some demonstration on land, and divert as much as possible the attention of the enemy from Farragut's operations. The bivouac of our Brigade was probably three miles east from the river, and some miles south from the outer line of fortifications of Port Hudson. The explosion of our gunboat Mississippi on the river, lighted up our camp with the glare of day, and the report which was not heard until the lapse of a minute, as it seemed, was terrific. This was about three o'clock in the morning, and an order coming nearly simultaneously, to fall in, and march back the way we came, created a temporary panic which is cursorily described in the verses which follow.

16. Colonel Chapin of the One Hundred and Sixteenth, New York, Commander of our Brigade, and, as is hinted, an inveterate driller thereof. He was a brave and faithful officer, and was killed at the storming of Port Hudson, on the 27th of May. President Lincoln appointed him Brigadier-General, of date the day of his death.

17. The Forty-Eighth Massachusetts, which, together with the One Hundred and Sixteenth New York, Twenty-First Maine, and our own Regiment, constituted our Brigade.

18. The old camp of the Forty-Eighth at Baton Rouge, had been very comfortably arranged, with elaborate cook-houses, &c., and that Regiment seemed to feel great apprehension, lest some other Regiment should arrive there first, and establish "squatter sovereignty."

19. Just as we came in sight of our old camp that day (the 15th,) we received orders to march back and encamp at Bayou Montesino.

20. We encamped on "Pike's Plantation," in a field where cane had been grown the year before. The furrows were very deep, and the rain soon filled them with water. Here we were nevertheless tired enough to sleep, but many a poor fellow contracted the fever that day and night, which, within a fortnight, consigned him to a furrow in which he still lies.

21. It was contrary to orders for any one to fire off a piece in camp, as false alarms were to be deprecated. One of our officers was under arrest for a week for firing off a pistol. The boys were sometimes *very sure* that their guns were so rusty that they wouldn't go off, and the cartridges couldn't be drawn with a wormer, and furthermore, an attack from the rebels was hourly expected. Yet if an unlucky private *tried* his piece, and it *did* go, he was summoned up in front of the Colonel's

quarters and ordered to do penance by standing there under arms till duly released. The musc records this as an instance of dilemmas in which soldiers were sometimes placed.

22. Lieutenant Colonel O'Brien of the Forty-Eighth Massachusetts, an impulsive, but brave Irishman, who commanded the storming party at Port Hudson, May 27, and was killed. On one occasion while at Bayou Montesino, he was officer of the day, and a Company of Rhode Island Cavalry who were out on picket, thought they discovered the enemy approaching, and reported accordingly to Colonel O'Brien, who rushed to Head-quarters, and made such representations, that Dudley's Brigade of our Division was ordered out to meet the intruders. It proved to be a false alarm.

23. "The French marched up the hill with an army of ten thousand men, and then—marched down again!"

24. Favorite expressions of astonishment with Frenchman "Jock," the Colonel's servant.

25. General Banks issued a congratulatory order, saying the object of our march was accomplished, &c., but as we had failed to capture Port Hudson, we could hardly "see the point."

26. On the 27th of May, the Forty-Ninth had one Company (G) on provost duty at Baton Rouge, Company F was guarding the baggage train; about one hundred men were on picket duty, and a large number in convalescent camp and hospital, so that but two hundred and thirty-three men took part in the assault. Of this number sixteen were killed and sixty-four wounded, making eighty in all, more than one-third of the whole number. The Colonel and Lieutenant Colonel were both wounded, and every Company had one or more officers killed or wounded. Officers and soldiers who served throughout the war, and who participated in the assault of May 27, have pronounced it one of the severest and bloodiest engagements in the history of the war.

APPENDIX.

THE REUNION.

THE REUNION of the officers of the Forty-Ninth Massachusetts, on the 21st of May, 1867, was a very gratifying occasion to the participants. A majority of the officers were present, but many were unavoidably kept away. At four o'clock in the afternoon, a business meeting was held for the purpose of establishing a more thorough organization for the future. After considerable discussion, it was voted to make it an Association of the honorably discharged members of the Regiment, including officers and privates, and articles of association were adopted, which are hereinafter published.

The Association then proceeded to the election of officers for the ensuing year, and made choice of the following:

President—Major CHARLES T. PLUNKETT.
Vice President—Captain HORACE D. TRAIN.
Treasurer—Captain CHARLES R. GARLICK.
Secretary—Lieutenant CHARLES W. KNIFFIN.

The remainder of the afternoon and evening was spent in social enjoyment, and the reviving of old camp memories. At nine o'clock in the evening, the officers present, and a number of invited guests sat down to a supper gotten up in the best style of Major Quackenboss, mine host of the American House. Lieutenant Colonel S. B. Sumner, the outgoing President of the Association, presided at the table, supported on the right by Major General Bartlett, Colonel of the Regiment, and on the left by Major Plunkett. After due justice had been done to the material part

of the feast, Colonel Sumner arose and remarked that it devolved upon
him to introduce the intellectual part of the entertainment. He said he
had come more than a hundred miles to be present at this gathering.
He alluded to the meeting held last January, to attend which, he with
several others had faithfully set out, but were blockaded by a snow-storm
before they could reach Pittsfield. They had waited in vain for two or
three days in hopes that Captain Weller, with his company of skirmishers,
might extricate them from their confinement at Lee, but at last they were
obliged to rely on their own resources, and reached Pittsfield afoot on a
fine Sunday morning, three days too late for a meeting with their old
comrades. It reminded him of the first attempt to take Port Hudson,
at which place they arrived—*almost!* Colonel S. then alluded, at some
length, to the circumstances of the present meeting. It was the anni-
versary of our first battle—at Plains Store. Just four years ago, we
were sleeping under the open sky, gazing up at the stars, having for the
first—most of us—experienced that day the sensation of being under fire,
and then indulging in lively anticipations of the morrow.

He alluded to the absent, reading letters from some, and explaining
the non-appearance of many of the others,—and some there were, said
he, who would never more meet with us, or any of their old comrades on
earth. After alluding in brief terms of eulogy to the gallant dead, and
particularly to the deceased officers, Deming, Judd, Reed, and Dresser,
Colonel S. proceeded to read the Poem which he had prepared for the
occasion, which was received with great enthusiasm.

The Chairman then stated that among the officers present was one
who had come a greater distance than himself to attend the meeting,
and who would be obliged to return home by the next train which was
due in half an hour, and he proposed to have him occupy that interval
by making a speech. He would therefore make no delay in calling out
Dr. Winsor, the old surgeon of the Forty-Ninth.

Dr. Winsor arose amid loud cheers. He said: Brethren of the Forty-
Ninth,—I think you count me as a Berkshire man to-night, though I was
born, bred, and have spent my days thus far in the eastern part of our
State. But if hearty sympathy, and service in common, and real affection count for anything, I am surely one with those whom I consider to

be about the best men in Berkshire. In my home down by Boston the name of the Forty-Ninth is a household word, held in dear and proud remembrance. My oldest boy, who believes "our Regiment" to be about the tip-top of creation,—his only experience of military life having been a fortnight at Snedekers—begged hard to come with me and see it once more.

I am delighted to be here to-night, meeting these old friends and renewing our old associations, and I consider myself very fortunate to have escaped all the outposts of business and made my way safely into your lines to-night.

It may not be without interest to you to hear how it happened that I, a stranger to every one of you, became the Surgeon of our Regiment. I think scarcely one of you know the facts. The Colonel and I had it pretty much to ourselves I believe. I was in charge of a hospital in Boston harbor, on Rainsford Island, during the early part of the war. My heart was as much in the cause as any man's, and many a time I raised the question with myself whether I ought not to join the army; and as often I answered that the time had not come for me to leave my family and my livelihood. The demand was not urgent to that degree. My business took me often to the State House, and Dr. Dale, the Surgeon General of the State, would now and then ask me why I did not take the surgeoncy of a regiment. My answer to him was the same as to myself, viz: that while there were enough competent unmarried men the time had not come for married men to leave their families. One day he urged me quite hard, and I answered him seriously: "Doctor, you know it isn't my duty to go now. If the time should come when no competent man can be found elsewhere, you may have a claim on me." He asked whether I would promise to respond to the call in case he could find no available competent man elsewhere, and I gave my word that under such circumstances I would go, Dr. Dale giving his word that he would not call on me till he had tried everywhere else. It was not long after this that he told me that the Forty-Ninth Massachusetts Regiment was under marching orders, and that he had sought everywhere for a surgeon, but in vain; and consequently he claimed the fulfillment of my promise. Of course I knew something about

Colonel Bartlett, and I remarked that he might like to have a voice in selecting his Regimental surgeon, and it would be as well to know how he felt about the proposed appointment. So Dr. Dale gave me a note of introduction, and furnished with this I looked up the Colonel at " Parker's." He received me politely of course, but was judiciously non-committal as he listened to my statement that I did not desire to go, and should be decidedly pleased to learn that there was some other man more to his liking who would go as Surgeon of his Regiment. We parted with the understanding that he would see Dr. Dale and that I should very soon be informed of his decision. I must say that I went away hoping that I had found far less favor in the eyes of Colonel Bartlett than he found in mine, a feeling, by the way, which I never entertained after I joined the Regiment. But next morning my appointment was sent me, and I proceeded to turn over a new leaf in my life. I resigned my place at the hospital, which I left as soon as my successor could come thither, and leaving my wife to attend to the thousand details involved in a change of homes, I left the dear old State and turned in search of the regiment of strangers with whom I was to serve the country, dearer to us than any State, and more precious than any home. Well, I found you in the gloomy, filthy barracks in Franklin street, made darker and nastier by the slop and clouds of a rainy November day, but I never saw there or elsewhere anything which shook my faith in the account I had heard at the State House in Boston, that the Forty-Ninth was made up of uncommonly good men ; and I was and have always been thankful that duty called me into that Regiment. Let me give my professional testimony to the good character of our Regiment. We had while in Baton Rouge more than the average amount of men on the sick-list, but it was not the result of dissipation or of anything like unwillingness to do duty ; it was partly because the malarious air of Louisiana was most strange and deadly to those whose native air was the pure breath of the Berkshire hills ; but I am sure it was quite as much because of the mental depression resulting from having nothing to do for the great cause, like what they proposed to themselves, when they left their pleasant homes and little farms among the mountains. The dull routine of those two and a half months at Baton Rouge—half camp life, half garrison duty—was far more irksome and dispiriting to them, than to most of the regiments in Augur's Division. Compare the Forty-Ninth with the rest of our brigade, and say whether separation from home and family and stupid waiting, waiting for the work, which we came out to do, was not a sorer trial to ours, than to the other regiments. I do believe, ours was the "bluest" and most homesick regiment in the Department of the Gulf. "Gloom" rested over us to an unusual degree, and it is a recognized fact, that a man depressed in spirits is the easiest prey to disease.

Don't understand me to imply that ours was a whining, mean-spirited Regiment. It was *true* blue, even when bluest. And where was there more regimental spirit? What I wish to point out is, that what was in the main our strength, was under certain circumstances our weakness. Those of us who were fortunate enough to continue at Port Hudson through the entire siege, know how much less sickness we had there, and how the men made light of real hardships. In the face of the enemy, their spirits rose and asserted their right to rule and use their bodies.

It hardly would be well or in the spirit of this occasion, for me to recall many of my professional experiences in the Forty-Ninth. What a man shares with the Surgeon, is for the most part hard—often terrible—to go through with, and painful to recall. And yet which of the memories of our short campaign are we willing to relinquish? Though they include the weariness and suffering of sickness and the hospital, the agony of wounds, the sad little funerals, with their dull drum beats, passing all too often along the dusty road; the hope deferred that made the heart sick, the yearning for home, and the doubt whether we should ever see it, or seeing it, should find its circle unbroken as we left it; which of all these would one of us let go? Did they not purchase for us the proud privilege of feeling that we have borne a man's part in our country's great struggle?

I give you, comrades, as a sentiment:

"The Memories of our Campaign—As precious as they are deeply graven."

The Chairman remarked that Dr. Winsor's statement of how he came to be connected with the Forty-Ninth was one of numberless instances of how curiously things are brought about in this world. And as another

illustration he would adduce the case of our old commander, who was a
Boston boy, an utter stranger to us all, but who happened to be sent to
Pittsfield as our post commandant, and eventually became our Colonel,
and who now owed to the Forty-Ninth all his present happy circumstances, domestic and otherwise. He called upon General Bartlett for
a speech.

General Bartlett premised by saying that he was not accustomed to
make speeches, except on drill and dress parade, and he should have
thought the Regiment had heard from him quite enough while they were
on duty. He was, however, greatly rejoiced to meet his old comrades
in arms, and although he had been identified with other regiments during the war, yet he found none which acquitted itself better, or for whose
officers he felt a more fraternal feeling. Although it was a nine months'
Regiment, yet he thought in point of soldierly qualities, it was equal to
any three years' regiment, which he had seen, and in respect to its social
peculiarities he thought it differed from most in this, that all its members,
officers and men seemed to have a brotherly feeling, and mutual regard
for each other, which did not and would not diminish. This arose from
the fact, that the men were all from the same county, and were mostly
of the substantial classes, less liable to become scattered and lose hold
of old associations. He said that while after the muster out of the
Forty-Ninth, he was serving in the Army of the Potomac, he heard fre-
quent complimentary allusions to his old Regiment the Forty-Ninth, and
was struck with the fact that it was so well remembered by men who had
served beside it in the Department of the Gulf. The General remarked
that he had become a son-in-law of Berkshire, having married one of
Berkshire's daughters—that he had become proprietor of a paper-mill in
the vicinity, and was looking forward to peaceful avocations and the
establishment of a permanent home in his adopted county. He continued his remarks at some length, and concluded amid hearty applause.

The Chairman next proposed the health of Major Plunkett, but desired
before calling him up, to say a few words about him. The Major and he
had tented and messed together during most of their campaign. They had
slept under the same blanket, and often divided the last crust, and had
numberless glees and glooms in common. It was a common remark

that if you wanted to know a man thoroughly, you should travel with him and see him away from home. He believed he had seen the Major under every possible circumstance, and found him ever the same genial, unselfish gentleman. As to his soldierly qualities, they needed no commendation here. After the Colonel and Lieutenant Colonel were wounded at Port Hudson, the command of the Regiment devolved upon the Major. How well he sustained the responsibility during the trying scenes that followed, through all the details of that long siege, and afterwards at Donelsonville, and finally in bringing the remnant of the Regiment safely home, all then present could testify. He hoped the Major would gratify his friends with a few remarks.

Major Plunkett arose with some reluctance, and exhibited considerable bashfulness for so big a boy. He said that he was not given to making speeches, but proceeded to belie the assertion by expressing in happy terms his gratification at meeting his brother officers. He had himself come quite a distance to be present on this occasion. He spoke in complimentary terms of his old comrade, Colonel Sumner, and concluded by moving that the Poem which had been read by him, be published in suitable form for distribution and preservation. The motion was carried.

The Chairman said it was about time to hear from the Quartermaster, and called upon Lieutenant Brewster to give some report from his department.

Quartermaster Brewster, responded at considerable length, and concluded by presenting the officers present with a portion all round of some of the original " hard tack " which he had brought home with him from the Department of the Gulf.

Hon. Henry Chickering of the Pittsfield Eagle, being present, was then introduced as one who had been a friend to the Forty-Ninth, and to the soldiers generally, and from whom some remarks would be very acceptable.

Mr. Chickering expressed himself greatly flattered by the invitation to sit at the festive board with the gallant officers of the Forty-Ninth, but felt himself hardly justified in taking time at so late an hour in making any remarks. He paid a high compliment to the Forty-Ninth, and said he had always felt a great pride in it as a Berkshire Regiment. He concluded with substantially the following sentiment:

"*The Forty-Ninth Regiment*—May its future career as an organization be as pleasant as its past has been glorious."

The Chairman then said that among the officers present, was one for whom all must feel peculiar emotions of regard and admiration. At the assault on Port Hudson, he was one of the officers of the "forlorn hope." Having been but newly commissioned as a Lieutenant, he volunteered to lead the storming party. He was borne from that bloody field with two bullet wounds, one in his breast, and the other a frightful one in the mouth and throat, fracturing the jaw into pieces, destroying the sight of one eye, and inflicting other injuries which would be a perpetual reminder to him of that terrible day. He was the worst wounded man of the Regiment who still lived. No one who saw him after the battle dared hope that he would ever return to Berkshire,—but it was ordered otherwise, and he was here to-night. And now, said the Chairman, I propose the health of Lieutenant THOMAS SIGGINS, of Company D., Great Barrington.

Lieutenant Siggins arose amid loud applause, and begged to be excused from making a speech. It was well known that his articulation was too imperfect to admit of it, and he would only say that he thanked his comrades for their flattering consideration.

At this time, there began to be numerous calls for Weller, and the Chairman apologized for having so far departed from military usage as to keep the skirmishers so long in the background. He remembered very well that when the Regiment were at the front, Captain Weller and his Company were apt to be deployed as skirmishers on every trying occasion. He would now call upon Captain Weller to narrate some of his experiences, to tell a story or sing a song, or better still, to do both.

Captain Weller, arose and proceeded to entertain the assembly for a half hour in his own inimitable style. He related his experience in the three months' campaign, and how General Butler came to find him out, and remember him ever afterwards as "that crazy Sergeant." The Captain also reviewed many incidents in the history of the Forty-Ninth, and told a succession of stories, which cannot be repeated with justice, but which kept the table in a roar.

Captain Garlick, as Commander of the Company on the left of the line, was next called out, and gracefully acknowledged the applause which greeted him, but excused himself from making any extended remarks.

The Chair then called attention to one officer present, who was wounded the 27th of May, and who subsequently occupied for several weeks the same ward with himself in the hospital at Baton Rouge. While lying there recovering from wounds, they had struck up an intimacy which he believed had been mutually pleasant,—on his own part, most certainly so. It had been their sad lot, to close the eyes of Lieutenant Judd, who occupied the same hospital ward, and who there died of his wounds. They had had common experiences which would make them friends and brothers always. He concluded by proposing the health of Lieutenant Charles W. Kniffin.

Lieutenant Kniffin responded at some length in his usual felicitous manner, but has failed to comply with the reporter's request for a sketch of his remarks.

The Chairman next introduced Lieutenant H. D. Sisson of Company E, as the officer who left a sick bed in hospital to go to the front, and whose conduct there was such as to establish his reputation as a brave and faithful officer.

Lieutenant Sisson said that while sitting there hearing the General remark upon the good qualities and honorable record of the Forty-Ninth, he could hardly restrain the rising question—how much are we indebted to our Colonel for all this? Every soldier knew that the best of men poorly officered, made poor soldiers. Therefore, if our Regiment stood in the fore-front of the Ninteenth Army Corps, it was because we had a soldier at our head. He would now propose: A health to General W. F. Bartlett. (Drank amid applause). Lieutenant S. continued: He believed it was usual, after a toast, for the giver to take his seat; but he would indulge in a few more remarks. Let us pause a few moments in our hilarity and bring up in our thoughts, recollections of a few chosen spirits who were once our comrades, but whom the Fates have taken, we trust, to a better realm. Let us mention some of their names—DEMING, JUDD,

REED, DRESSER. Inasmuch as we cannot enjoy their presence here, let us who survive, ever remember in our narration of past incidents, the noble part performed by these much honored comrades. Some might think it inappropriate in the midst of social rejoicing, to bring up thoughts of those who have passed the Rubicon between this world and the next, and are now dwelling in the fields of immortality. "But comrades," said Lieutenant S., "I am in one sense a believer in the proverb, 'whatever is, is right.' I believe as did President Lincoln, that, should the sun, on one of these beautiful spring days, be stayed in its course, in mid-heaven, and all of this broad country from the shores of the Orient to the Occident be made to bloom in perpetual spring, it would be no surer indication of a direct interposition of Providence for our great good, than was the Great Rebellion, with its accompanying train of consequences. Is it not right then, that we, who were the instruments by which the deepest, darkest, most damning curse that ever blighted humanity has been obliterated—we, who have helped make permanent the most perfect human government the sun ever shone upon—we, who have linked ourselves together by that welding process that eliminates the dross, hypocrisy, and unites the better qualities in an unalloyed union, —is it not right that we should occasionally release our hold on the every day duties of life, and give our convivial feelings loose rein,—and is it not right that at the same time we should keep fresh in mind the memories of those who have passed before us? Allow me again to propose as a toast:

"The Wife, the Children, the Father, the Mother, the Sisters of the Fallen Soldier."

The Chair then stated that Company G of Adams, was represented this evening by Lieutenant H. M. Lyons; Company G immediately on the arrival of the Regiment at Baton Rouge was detailed for provost duty, and was kept at that work until the Regiment returned North. It was therefore, unable to participate in any of the battles, but its good conduct while on provost duty, had been a subject of remark among military men in the Nineteenth Army Corps, and reflected credit upon the Regiment.

Lieutenant Lyons responded, saying that the officers would bear witness with what reluctance Company G having set out with the Regiment for Port Hudson, obeyed the order to return to Baton Rouge and resume provost duty. The Lieutenant in fitting terms proceeded to testify to his affection for the old Regiment, and his happiness at participating in the greetings of the occasion.

Captain Lingenfelter of Company C was then introduced, as the only officer of the Regiment who could boast of having risen from the post of a Sergeant to that of Captain during the campaign of the Forty-Ninth. The Captain replied with a few happy remarks.

Colonel Sumner said that he desired next to call out Lieutenant F. A. Francis of Company A, one of the wounded on the memorable 27th of May, and acting Adjutant of the Regiment from that time until the muster out. He would like to acknowledge his personal obligations to Lieutenant Francis, for services rendered in trading off his (Colonel Sumner's) fractious horse, with one of Grierson's Cavalry officers, for the renowned steed "Dick Robinson." This sally provoked considerable merriment with the officers who knew the circumstances of the "swap." Lieutenant Francis made a brief and modest response.

Lieutenant Kellogg of Company I, was next brought to his feet, and made a five minute speech, stating that sickness in his family had induced him to send in his resignation before the Regiment was ordered into action, but as the attack on Port Hudson took place before he left the Department of the Gulf, he was on hand, and went in to the fight "on his own hook." It fell to his lot to bring some of the wounded men off the field, as some who were present would remember.

The Chairman then introduced Lieutenant R. C. Taft of Company K, alluding in complimentary terms to the energy and skill displayed by that officer in recruiting and organizing his Company to fill out the quota of the Regiment. Lieutenant Taft said that he had depended upon Captain Weston to speak for Company K on this occasion, but the Captain had been obliged to leave the table in order to take the train east at half-past eleven. Company K however, could speak for itself, as the record showed that it had a larger list of killed and wounded on the 27th of May, than any other Company. It was not his fortune, owing to ill health, to remain with the Regiment during its whole term of service, but his connection with it was among the pleasantest of his past experiences.

Brief remarks followed from W. R. Plunkett Esq., and other invited guests, after which a variety of informal speeches, toasts, sentiments and stories became the order of the night, and the assembly broke up in the "wee sma' hours," with a toast to absent comrades, and cheers for the OLD FORTY-NINTH.

ARTICLES OF ASSOCIATION

OF THE ASSOCIATION OF THE OFFICERS AND MEN OF THE

FORTY-NINTH MASSACHUSETTS VOLUNTEERS.

---

1. THIS Association shall be called "The Association of the Officers and Men, of the Forty-Ninth Regiment Massachusetts Volunteers."

2. The object of this Association shall be the holding of an Annual Reunion of the surviving Officers and Men of the Forty-Ninth Regiment, for the purpose of rendering some annual tribute to the memory of fallen comrades ; of reviving old associations, and brightening the chain which unites us in peculiar relations of sympathy and friendship.

3. The regular members of said Association shall consist of the surviving Officers and Men of the Forty-Ninth Regiment of Massachusetts Volunteers, who served in the war for the suppression of the rebellion, and were honorably discharged, and who shall comply with the requirements set forth in these articles.

4. The officers of the Association, shall consist of a President, Vice President, Treasurer and Secretary, who shall perform the ordinary duties of such offices, and who shall also constitute an Executive Committee, and shall be chosen annually.

5. Every member shall pay annually to the Treasurer, at or before the annual meeting, the sum of five dollars, and such other assessment as for contingent purposes may be voted by the members, or determined upon by the Executive Committee, not exceeding the sum of five dollars annually.

6. Said Association shall meet at least annually at such time and place as shall be determined upon by the members at the next preceding meeting: *Provided*, that the Executive Committee, when in their judgment any contingency requires a change of time, may make such change of time, upon giving all the members due and seasonable notice.

7. Honorary members may be elected at annual meetings by a majority vote of the regular members present.

8. On the day of each annual Reunion, a business meeting shall be holden at 4 P. M., at a place to be designated and provided by the Executive Committee, at which time all the business affairs of the Association shall be transacted. In the evening of the same day, there shall be an Annual Supper, provided under the direction of the Executive Committee, at which the members, regular and honorary, and invited guests may be present.

9. The name of any member of the Association failing to comply with these articles, may be stricken from the roll, by a two-thirds vote of the members present at any annual meeting.

10. These articles may be amended at any annual business meeting, by a majority vote of members present.

www.ingramcontent.com/pod-product-compliance
Lightning Source LLC
Chambersburg PA
CBHW030913260626
47169CB00008B/2832